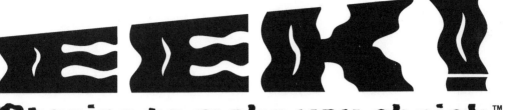

Stories to make you shriek™

For Beginning Re:
Ages 6-8

This series of spooky stories has been created especially for beginning readers—children in first and second grades who are developing their reading skills.

How do these books help children learn to read?

- Kids love creepy stories and these stories are true page-turners (but never too scary).
- The sentences are short.
- The words are simple and repeated often in the story.
- The type is large with lots of room between words and lines.
- Full-color pictures on every page act as visual "clues" to help children figure out the words on the page.

Once children have read one story, they'll be asking for more!

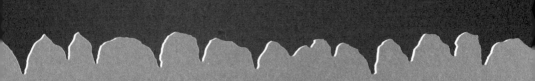

Library of Congress Cataloging-in-Publication Data

Dussling, Jennifer.
    Creep show / by Jennifer Dussling ; illustrated by Jeff Spackman.
       p.   cm. — (Eek! Stories to make you shriek)
    Summary: Even though he tries to stay away, a boy keeps going back to an old theater
where he is drawn into increasingly dangerous movies.
    [1. Motion pictures—Fiction.   2. Horror stories.]   I. Spackman, Jeff, ill.
II. Title.   III. Series.
PZ7.D943Cr   1996
[Fic]—dc20   95-18331
                                                                        CIP
ISBN 0-448-41272-1   A B C D E F G H I J   AC

sy-to-Read
es 6–8

EEK!

Stories to make you shriek ™

Creep Show

By Jennifer Dussling

Illustrated by Jeff Spackman

Grosset & Dunlap • New York

Kids stay away from

the old Star Movie Palace.

The story is that

some guy died in there.

He got scared to death

from a horror movie.

I don't know if it's true or not.

But the Star gives me the creeps.

I have to pass it every day

on my way home.

I always walk on the other side

of the street.

But today I saw a sign out front—

FREE MOVIE TODAY.

A free movie!

Was this for real?

I crossed the street to get a closer look.

The movie was called Fly Ball.

I had never heard of it.

But I love baseball.

And I love baseball movies.

This was too good to pass up.

I started to push the door.

But it swung open—

all by itself!

Weird.

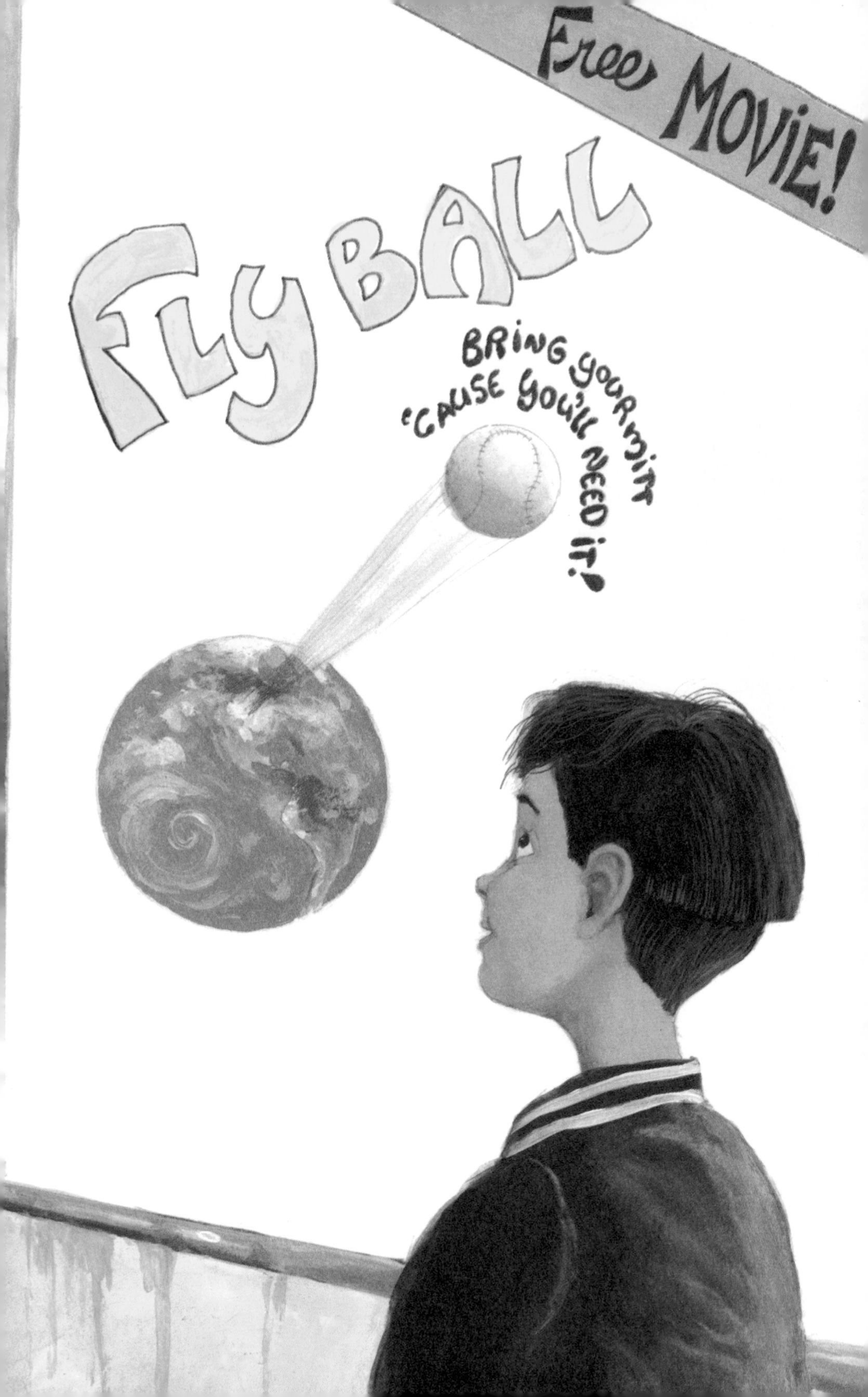
Free MOVIE!
FLY BALL
BRING YOUR MITT
'CAUSE YOU'LL NEED IT!

Inside it was dark and spooky.

All the seats were very dusty.

You would think with a free movie

the place would be packed.

But no one else was there—

just me.

A bag of popcorn was by

one of the seats.

It was like it was put there

just for me.

Then the movie started.

It was about a Little League team.

They weren't any good—

just like my team!

The coach was yelling something

at a kid in right field.

I play right field too.

The kid turned around.

It was me!

All of a sudden,

there was a WHOOOSH!

And I felt dizzy.

I shook my head and looked around.

I was at a ballpark,

standing in right field!

I was not watching a movie anymore.

I was <u>in</u> the movie!

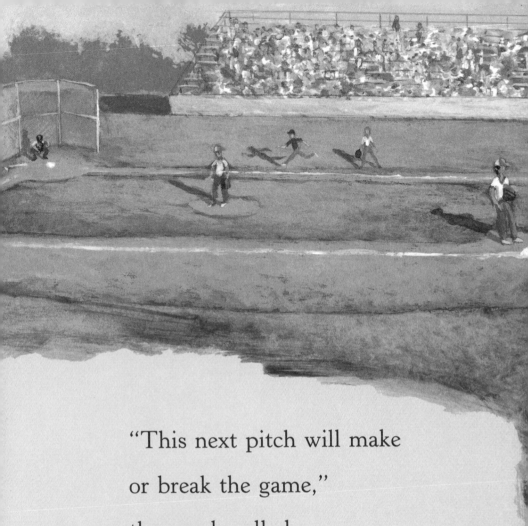

"This next pitch will make

or break the game,"

the coach yelled.

CRACK!

The batter smacked the ball

into right field.

It was just the kind of ball

I never get.

But this time I dove across the grass.

I reached out my glove.

I stretched.

And I caught it!

The final out!

I saved the game!

It was my dream come true.

Kids lifted me up.

Everybody was cheering.

Then the lights came on.

I blinked.

I was back in the theater.

Back in my seat.

I walked out in a daze.

Had this really happened?

I started walking home.

Then I noticed it.

There were grass stains on my jeans!

The next day at school
I started to tell my friends
about the Star.
But I stopped.

They probably would think I was nuts.

And somehow I felt

this was <u>my</u> secret.

Somehow this was meant just for me.

That afternoon I had a piano lesson.

So I couldn't go to the Star.

But the next day I went back.

Was there going to be another free movie?

Yes!

The movie was called Surf's Up!

I have always wanted to surf.

I knew I should go home.

I had a ton of homework.

But I felt like the Star

was pulling me—

like a magnet.

I had to see if I was going to be

<u>in</u> the movie again.

I went inside.

This time there was a Mallo-Nut

on one of the seats.

Mallo-Nuts are my favorite candy bars!

It really <u>was</u> put there just for me!

Then the movie started.

It was about surfers.

They were watching another kid surf.

They said how cool he looked.

I got a tingly feeling.

I was pretty sure

I knew who they were

talking about.

Me!

WHOOOOSH!

Like magic, I was in

the movie again.

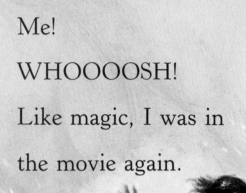

It was like I had been surfing

my whole life.

But all of a sudden

a huge wave knocked me

off my surfboard!

I wiped out!

Over and over

I tumbled in the water.

My arm scraped across my board.

Ow!

That hurt!

I struggled out of the water.

But what do you know?

I wasn't at the beach anymore!

I was back in the theater—

back in my seat.

What was going on here?

I ran out of the theater

and down the street.

Then I passed a store window

and stopped.

I saw myself in the glass.

My hair was wet.

And I had a sunburn.

How could I get a sunburn

from a movie?

But it <u>was</u> a sunburn.

And it hurt.

My arm hurt too.

I didn't want to look at it.

I didn't want to see

what I knew I would see.

There were cuts and scrapes

from my wipe-out.

Uh-oh.

This was a little scary.

Maybe more than a little scary.

I got a sunburn in a dark theater.

I cut up my arm.

I got <u>hurt</u> in a <u>movie</u>.

And it was only a surf movie!

What if it had been a murder mystery?

Or a war story?

Or a western?

Or, worst of all, a horror movie?

I ran all the way home.

I didn't stop until I got to my room.

I was scared.

There was no way

I was going back to the Star.

Who knew what could happen

next time?

At dinner

my mom looked at me funny.

"Gosh, your face is red,"

she said.

"You must have a fever.

No school for you tomorrow."

So the next day I stayed home.

No school is usually great.

Not this time.

I tried to read a book.

I tried to play a video game.

But all I could think about was the Star.

After lunch my mom went shopping.

I was all alone.

Uh-oh.

I tried not to go.

But something was pulling me—

pulling me to the Star.

I grabbed my coat.

In ten minutes I was there.

The poster today said

The Candy Factory.

Now that sounded like fun!

The worst thing that

could happen to me was a bellyache!

At my seat were two Mallo-Nuts.

And a big cherry soda.

When I sat down,

I thought I heard the door lock.

Weird.

Then the curtain went up.

But wait!

What was that sign

on the screen?

The Candy Factory

will not be shown today.

Instead today's movie is—

KILLER SPIDERS FROM MARS

Oh, no!

I had to get out!

I ran to the door.

It <u>was</u> locked!

Slowly, I turned around.

The movie was starting and

WHOOOOOSH!

I was in it.

The ground started to shake.

What was that?

Then I saw them—

really big, green spiders

with really big fangs!

They were coming toward me!

I started to run.

Maybe I would be lucky.

Maybe I could get away.

Maybe this wasn't . . .

the end.